T0194021

Adventures of Jack, a Little 4 by 4

Maggie Hopkins

AuthorHouse™
1663 Liberty Drive
Bloomington, IN 47403
www.authorhouse.com
Phone: 1 (800) 839-8640

Because of the dynamic nature of the Internet, any web addresses or links contained in this book may have changed since publication and may no longer be valid. The views expressed in this work are solely those of the author and do not necessarily reflect the views of the publisher, and the publisher hereby disclaims any responsibility for them.

This book is printed on acid-free paper.

ISBN: 978-1-7283-6869-6 (sc)
ISBN: 978-1-7283-6870-2 (e)

Print information available on the last page.

Published by AuthorHouse 08/10/2020

authorHOUSE®

Adventures of Jack, a Little 4 by 4

Jack was a proud and happy little 4 by 4.

His shiny new orange paint shone in the sun. He had 4 knubby new wheels.

His brave little engine heart purred with excitement. He was taking his family for their first adventure in the country.

Mom and Dad, little Jamie and baby Joey.

Grandma was coming too.

Two huge black dogs, Lucy and Lola joined the happy family.

Let's go. Let's go.

He tooted.

With a mighty heave and a puff of smoke,

They were on their way.

They passed a farm with a big red barn.

The cows mooed.

The horses ran along the fence.

Such a happy day.

The sun shone brightly.

No clouds in the sky.

They bounced down the country roads to the mountains.

Jack was proud to be such a strong and brave little 4 by 4.

He would keep his family safe.

He bounced through the potholes in the road.

He climbed all the hills.

He crossed all the creeks and streams.

Finally they were in the mountains.

Nothing could stop Jack now.

He went faster and faster.

No pothole was too big.

No hill or mountain was too high.

No stream or river was too wide or too deep.

Jack was so proud.

He could do it all.

The sun was dipping over the edge of the mountains.

Right ahead of him, across a creek, rose a big hill.

The biggest one yet.

He could climb it.

He was the toughest, bravest little 4 by 4 ever.

With a shift of his gear, and a mighty rev of his little engine heart,

He rushed towards the water.

His family squealed.

The dogs howled.

Grandma covered her eyes.

WHOOSH!

He hit the water.

Spinning his wheels, he crashed along.

The river was too deep and wide.

Down the river they went. Twisting and turning.

Bobbing up and down.

They were in a 4 by 4 boat.

Around and around they went.

Then, CRASH!

He stopped with a jerk.

He was stuck on a huge rock in the middle of the river.

Water was rushing around the doors and fenders.

His family was not happy.

Baby Joey was crying.

Dogs were barking.

Quickly, Dad came to the rescue.

Climbed out the window.

Carried his family to safety on the bank of the river.

The dogs swam too.

It was almost dark.

Dad made a fire.

The family huddled together all night.

In the morning, his family started walking.

They were cold and hungry.

The nearest town was many miles away.

Jack watched them leave.

He was all alone now.

Jack was so ashamed.

He though his little engine heart would break.

Tears ran down his little grill face.

High up in the mountains miles away, rain had begun to fall.

The creeks and streams flowed down the mountainside.

The rivers below began to rise.

Little by little the water around Jack got deeper.

He was lifted off the huge rock.

He was FREE!

He spun his four knubby wheels.

Narrowed his little headlight eyes.

With all the bravery and strength left his little angel heart.

He spun across the river to safety.
His tin body shook with happiness.
Up the slippery bank of the river.
Over the grassy meadow.
Down the twisty hill.
He had to find his family.
Up over the hill came Jacki
There they were, SAFE!
He was so happy.
He was wet and dirty.
His bright and orange fenders were dented and bent.
But he was here!
TOOT! TOOT! TOOT!
He blinked his headlights.
They climbed in.
They were so happy to see him.
Mom and Dad, Little Jamie and baby Joey. Grandma too.
The dog jumped for Joy.
He whisked them quickly and safely down the bumpy road to town.
All was well that night.

Everyone was fine.

After a warm mean and a hot bath.

Of course.

"OUR LITTLE HERO."

Had a wash and shine

It had been a hard lesson for Jack our little hero in the end,

Never again would he be such a show off and lead his family into danger.

UNTIL NEXT TIME!

Printed in the United States
By Bookmasters